C0-AWT-772

# Catch of the Day

## A Newfound Lake Cozy Mystery
### Book 1

Virginia K. Bennett

**Copyright © 2023 by Virginia K. Bennett**

All rights reserved. Published by Virginia K. Bennett.

No part of this book may be reproduced in any form or by any electronic or mechanical means, including information storage and retrieval systems, without written permission from the author, except for the use of brief quotations in a book review.

This is a work of fiction. Names, characters, places, and incidents either are the products of the author's imagination or are used fictitiously. Any resemblance to actual persons, living or dead, events, or locales is entirely coincidental.

Cover by Pixel Squirrel Studio

*To the members of the writing community who supported me early on, thank you!*

*Skye Jones*
*Marissa Farrar*
*Dawn Edwards*
*Kat Reads Romance*
*Kathryn LeBlanc*
*TL Swan*
*VR Tennent*
*Gina Sturino*
*Rachelle Kampen*
*...and so many more!*

# Table of Contents

# Chapter 1

## *The Catch*

"THAT'S NOT WHAT I MEANT WHEN I NAMED THE place." Ben's attempt at humor was lost on those watching the search and rescue team retrieve a body found floating at the foot of the lake. Gawkers stood on the opposite side of the road adjacent to the small beach, just in front of his restaurant, The Catch of the Day. While the restaurant was practically in the lake, none of the seafood favored by the local patrons was caught there. Ben was a food snob, and all the seafood he served was driven up from the coast four days a week – fresh as could be for middle New England.

Ben inherited a piece of land from his grandfather at the foot of Newfound, cleanest lake in New Hampshire, and decided to build an open-air restaurant for tourists and locals to enjoy with high-quality seafood and a stunning view of the water. Locals wished there were more "local prices" but enjoyed the bar and takeout as much as the visitors. Seating was limited and in high demand during the peak of summer. Unfortunately for Ben, the restaurant had been packed with a line around the building for take out when a scream was heard from an approaching boat.

Police arrived within five minutes of the report, but search and rescue took another ten. Librarian Rebecca Ramsey watched the divers retrieve the body and remove it from the area by RHIB - Rigid Hull Inflatable Boat. She was sitting on the deck, covered from the sun by an awning, enjoying her fried scallops and onion rings when she heard the scream. A young girl was seen moments later with a cell phone to her ear, presumably calling 9-1-1. Rebecca jumped up to see what the issue was.

"Excuse me." Rebecca gently placed her hand on the arm of the moving waitress. "Do you know what that girl was screaming about?" When the waitress stopped and turned to look at her, she realized it was Molly, a high school classmate. "Oh, hey, Molly. Any idea what's going on?"

"No. But it looks like people are starting to gather." Molly motioned in the direction of the parking area with her elbow then rushed off with dirty dishes destined for the dishwasher.

Rebecca stood to check out who was gathering. She couldn't see much from her spot on the deck, so she walked over to the group surrounding the owner.

Ben was pointing and chatting up the group currently focused on the water. "All I could see was a large body and short hair." His description lacked detail because the body was quite a distance away and was now out of sight; only divers and police in boats remained visible. "Well, time to get back to work and back to lunch!" His mind was clearly back on running a business while the potential patrons were all discussing theories on who it might be. Rebecca's mind was divided – go back for the fried food or onto the dock where a police boat was about to tie up. The food could wait.

"Hey, Chief Towne," Rebecca called out after the engine noise died down. Kenny Towne had been a love interest in middle school, but was now a divorcee, dad of two and a good friend.

"Rebecca, call me Kenny, would ya."

"Not while you're in uniform at the scene of what I assume to be a crime."

"You're not digging for clues already, are you?" Chief Towne knew Rebecca too well. Always one to be nearby when a mystery might need to be solved, Rebecca had developed a certain reputation in town. Not a bad reputation, mind you, but one that preceded her. Rebecca's years in the library meant that she had read her fair share of true-crime books and criminal fiction.

"Why would you ask that? I was simply minding my own business, eating some seafood on a lovely Sunday afternoon when you showed up, lights flashing, interrupting my meal. The fact that I happen to be here on the dock with you after you pulled a body out of the water is pure coincidence." She smiled a small half-smile on one side of her mouth while tucking a length of straight auburn hair behind her ear and looking up at the puffy white clouds floating in a blue sky. Rocking back on her flip-flopped heels, she continued, "Might you have any information to share...like whose body it is?"

"Rebecca, you know that isn't public knowledge until we notify next of kin." The way he said her name sounded like he both wanted to tell her what she was asking for and regretted having to say no. The way he looked at her spoke volumes. Rebecca was even more stunning now than she was in high school. She had a relaxed style that looked effortless even though she put a lot of thought into it. Most of her tops were somehow related to being a librarian or lover of books in general, but she paired them with just the right jeans, boots, cardigans and sandals that she looked like a Facebook ad for those companies that mails outfits to you.

"Well, can you tell me if it's a local or a tourist?" Kenny's eyes scanned her outfit today. Vertically, her shirt read, 'The Book Was Better,' with wing-framed glasses in place of the middle letters in the word book. He chuckled while trying to look off to the side before regaining eye contact.

"I can tell you that I knew exactly who it was the moment I saw the body. Looks like it's been in the water since last night, but you didn't hear that from me."

Making a motion to zip her lips, Rebecca nodded. "Your limited and not-very-useful secret is safe with me."

"I've got to get going, but it was good to see you. Guess I'll be seeing even more of you than normal, huh?" Chief Towne, Kenny, removed his hat and wiped his brow. The summer sun was hot today, and the time spent on the water in full uniform was starting to get to him.

His hair was matted due to the heat and sweat, but he still had a full head of thick locks, just like over twenty years ago in high school. When it wasn't under his hat all day, Kenny still looked like he could be in a shampoo commercial from the 80's – silky and just the perfect single shade of brown that male models attempted to get from a bottle.

"I would say that has a high probability, Chief." Rebecca and Chief Towne headed up toward The Catch of the Day. Rebecca walked back toward her table, and Chief Towne made his way to a patrol car blocking those who were trying to get some information about what happened. "See you later." She waved and looked over her shoulder with a full smile this time.

As Rebecca returned to her table, she noticed that her meal still sat half eaten. Most tables had emptied but hadn't been cleared yet, so she sat down to see if the scallops were still any good. Nope. Cool and soggy, the remainder of the seafood and onion rings went uneaten. She left cash on the table, enough to cover the bill and tip from memory, because she ate this same meal so often during the short season the restaurant was open. "Molly, cash is on the table. Could you let my waitress know?" Summer help had started, and that included people only around from June to August. She didn't yet know her waitress's name.

"Sure thing," Molly replied, busily carrying a tray that looked like it weighed more than she did to the staff door at the back of the building. Molly had been a friend in high school, but an acquaintance only once Rebecca finished college. Molly left for school but never finished. She moved around from place to place but settled back in the Newfound area many years ago. While they didn't spend time together outside of the diner/server relationship they had, there was still a long-lasting familiarity between them. The only big change for Molly was the length of her hair. The deep brown hair that once flowed in bouncy curls was now in a very short pixie-cut style. She had a petite frame and face, so it didn't really matter what haircut she went with, and this one suited her just as well as the high-school length.

Still hungry, Rebecca went to the ice cream window to get a small dish of chocolate chip cookie dough. Considering it had been invented during her childhood only a few hours away in Burlington, Vermont, it was a standard order in the summer. "Two scoops of cookie dough, please, in a dish." The teenager inside the window hollered to another teenager to scoop the flavor ordered by the amateur sleuth. Rebecca observed the variety of hair colors between the two girls working and wondered if it was on purpose or an accident that they could just about cover the whole color spectrum between the pair of them. Cash traded hands, and Rebecca accepted the white Styrofoam dish of deliciousness.

She just couldn't stop herself from asking the manager if he saw anything she missed. "Ben, got a second?" Ben turned and frowned upon seeing it was Rebecca calling his name. The reputation did precede her, and Ben did not look happy to see the possible list of questions walking in his direction.

"Pretty busy here with the disruption and being short-staffed today. What can I do for you?" He looked at Rebecca and scanned the potential patrons now dispersing from the area since most of the action had moved on. He looked nervous that people who were planning to eat had now changed their minds. Ben went to a prestigious school for business management, so the business was always front and center for him. He worked in major cities for several years following college and, like many others before him, returned to live in the Newfound area as an adult. If you squinted a little, he looked like a grown-up version of Fred Savage. Clearly Fred Savage *had* grown up, but many still thought of him from his roles on TV and as the sick kid from The Princess Bride.

There really was no better place to grow up than rural New Hampshire, and many locals returned when it was time to start a family or buy a vacation home. Ben had been close once or twice, but never committed to becoming a family man. He was always too focused on whatever job he currently held. He continued to scan the few stragglers that remained, hoping a couple might come back to eat.

"Just wanted to see if you knew anything about the body they pulled out." Rebecca attempted to gain his attention.

"No more than anyone else. They were too far away to really see anything. I've got to get back to helping the staff get the tables reset. Did you eat already?" Always looking out for the best interests of the restaurant, and not necessarily with his eyes, he didn't notice the ice cream in her hands.

"I ate some but left to see what all the commotion was about. The ice cream will have to be enough for now."

"Well, I'm sure I'll see you around again soon. Gotta go." And with that, Ben walked back into the restaurant, fingers running through his thick, jet black hair.

Rebecca kicked off her flip flops and deposited them on the driver's side floor of her green Subaru. Barefoot now, she walked across the small one-way street to the beach, dish in one hand, spoon in the other. She sat on the boulders that separated the road from the beach and watched waves lap the edge of the shore. Boats passed by towing tubers and skiers in equal measure. She pondered a mental list of where to start her *investigation,* considering she had so little information to go on while she pulled a stray hair from her face, returning it to the spot behind her ear. "Well, I guess I'll have to talk to Kenny. They say food is the way to a man's stomach, so I'll start there." After she finished talking to herself and eating the ice cream, she drove to the local grocery store for supplies.

# Chapter 2

## *The Details*

THE LOCAL GROCERY STORE PARKING LOT WAS BUSY, even for a Sunday, but the library was closed, so today was as good a day as any to pick up the necessary ingredients to get Kenny talking. Strawberries were in season, so Rebecca decided she would go up to Plymouth to pick up fresh ones at the farm stand, if she could get the grocery shopping done quickly.

The automatic doors slid open, revealing the same carts that had been around for as long as she could remember – she may have even been pushed in one as a child. If it were just a little later in the summer, she'd go to Walker Farm for fresher ingredients, but farms in New Hampshire took a while to catch up with the summer rush. The taste and smell of sweet corn swirled in her mind while she looked through the trucked-in produce she had to choose from, but only for a little longer.

Rebecca picked up things here and there before

approaching the meat coolers for ground beef, ground lamb and ground pork. Pasta with meatballs was the answer to the question she had been pondering since leaving the beach. Monday was predicted to be cooler with a bit of a drizzle, so sauce and meatballs in a crockpot were perfect. When Kenny arrived, she'd only need to prep the pasta and a side salad. All checked out, she made her way to her car and drove first to Plymouth then home to make the call that would hopefully lead her to some answers about the body pulled from the lake.

While putting away groceries, including those fresh strawberries she was daydreaming about, the phone rang and rang on speaker until finally she was forced to leave a message. "Hey, Kenny, wanted to know if you'd like to have dinner tomorrow night and talk about whatever you might be allowed to talk about. Let me know. Bye." She pressed the button to end the call. It wasn't surprising that only a few hours after finding a person involuntarily floating a couple hundred feet from shore, Kenny was too busy to answer his personal phone.

Rebecca had been there for Kenny when he was a gawky teenager, a lovestruck newlywed, a glowing new father and a heartbroken divorcee. They knew everything there was to know about each other, and that included a friendship that could survive anything. After his marriage ended, Rebecca felt he needed to be looked after by someone who knew him best. She'd invited him over for meals once a week or so, regularly over the past year, carefully arranged around when he didn't have his kids.

He and his ex worked hard to provide the best situation possible for their two girls. There was no set schedule. Each week, they looked at his work duties and the school schedule to decide what would be best for the kids. If only all divorces could work out this smoothly, kids wouldn't have to suffer for their parents' decisions.

While at Rebecca's house, she and Kenny often played board games and watched movies together. However, Rebecca was the cook. Kenny was happy to supply the comedic relief and dramatic details of his job – when allowed.

The phone vibrated on the counter, signaling a message.

Kenny: 6:30 tomorrow work for you?

Rebecca: Library closes at 6pm...dinner for 7?

Kenny: See you then.

That was easy. Tomorrow night was enough time for him to collect more information and for her sauce to cook in the crockpot after a quick stop home during her lunch break. Now, what to do with the strawberries? "Strawberry shortcake." If only she thought about it at the store, she would have purchased biscuits. "Good thing I have enough time to make them tonight," she told her cats, Joey and Bean. They already had the names when she adopted them from the shelter, and she couldn't bring herself to change them. Shelter staff estimated they were around six or seven months old at the time but had been at the shelter nearly four of those months after being surrendered together. Black cats were harder to adopt out

– something about superstitions and fur on clothing. Clearly, Rebecca didn't care about either of those because she adopted them after not even seeing Joey. They belonged together, and she was just the person to love them unconditionally. She used May first as their birthday, so they were currently just over one.

Ingredients were now flying to the counter from cabinets and shelves, slated to become biscuits – the only New England way to serve a strawberry shortcake as far as she was concerned. In what seemed like no time at all, she had six large biscuits on a lightly greased baking sheet heading into a 425°F oven. "Tomorrow, I'll let you two lick the beaters for the whipped cream." It was almost cruel to tell them anything that included the word cream and then not give them cream, so she was able to get the circling furballs around her legs to stop by bribing them with treats. "Can't forget the bowl and beaters." Even though they didn't care, she liked to talk to her fur babies like they did. She retrieved a medium-size metal bowl from a cabinet and the necessary beaters for the electric hand mixer and placed them in the freezer to chill. Joey and Bean didn't benefit from this process, so they relocated to the living room once the treats were gone.

Now she had to sit down and collect a mental list of everything she knew and everything she wanted to know by the end of tomorrow's dinner. Joey had already claimed the comfy chair in the corner, so Rebecca would share the couch. Bean was a good cat who snuggled right up next to her hip when she sat down. While stroking

Bean's back she said, "We need to find out who was removed from the lake if possible. Hopefully the next of kin has already been notified so Kenny can tell us. Also, we need to think about why anyone would murder him or her, assuming it was murder. I guess this all could have been just a horrible accident. People have been known to go out boating at night and fall in." She grimaced at the thought of falling into Newfound at night.

Newfound in June was still very cold. Due to the number of sources feeding the lake, the water turned over about four times per year – one of the reasons it was so clean. There also hadn't been enough warm days yet to make much of a difference in the water temperature. The lake was impressively deep in places, so it stayed pretty cold, even into August.

"Second," she continued her synopsis in Bean's direction, "we need to see if Kenny has any suspects." Suspects were going to be difficult to come by if this had been a tourist, so she was pleased Kenny hinted he recognized the body. Rebecca would be off the job if it wasn't someone who had permanent ties to the area. "Drowning has got to be an awful way to go, unless the lake was part of a plan to dispose of a body not actually kill the person." Bean peacefully purred next to her leg, not a care in the world about bodies of water so long as she wasn't being forced into one.

Rebecca paused for a moment, remembering who was there when the body was being recovered. Obviously, Ben, the manager, had been there trying to keep things light. He appeared nervous, scanning the crowd, making witty comments to cover the feelings his face and body language gave away. There were several locals in and around the restaurant, but many more unfamiliar faces were getting ready to head back to their real lives, enjoying one last lunch by the water before hopping in their expensive SUVs to travel south on I-93. She also had spoken to Molly, the waitress, who said she didn't know what was going on. Did she look busy or was she stressed about something else?

"Well, we're not going to get very far tonight. I'll take the biscuits out to cool before bed and put a bag of frozen strawberries in the fridge too." She stood, waking Bean who remained on the couch but gave a long stretch and then crisscrossed her adorable front paws over her face. Joey didn't move, and he remained asleep on the comfy chair. Rebecca made her way to the kitchen to check the time left on the timer. Just two minutes remained. She transferred the bag of frozen strawberries to the fridge to thaw. It was a family secret to add the frozen strawberries because it gave two different textures and added lots of juice to the biscuits. After watching the final seconds tick down on the timer, she removed the tray from the oven. The biscuits were carefully moved to the cooling rack, and she went upstairs to get ready for bed.

Rebecca watched one episode of Cutthroat Kitchen before heading back downstairs to transfer the cooled biscuits to a container – no one puts warm biscuits in a closed container. As she crawled into bed, her mind reeled with possibilities of what might have happened

Saturday night or early Sunday morning...or maybe much earlier. She hadn't even considered that this might be a crime or accident that happened way before this weekend. Oh, the things she had to discuss with Kenny tomorrow night. How would she ever make it through a whole day working in the library?

# Chapter 3

## *The Chief*

As expected, Rebecca watched the clock all morning – clocks, that is. She never noticed just how many clocks were in the library before today: two analog, three digital, a sundial in the front garden and her phone's lock screen. There was even a clock on the thermostat. Apparently, all eight were broken because they weren't moving! She checked the clock after finishing her morning OJ, assuming it was at least 10:30am – 10:07am! How was it only 10:07am? She knew this dinner was consuming her thoughts, but this was next level.

The library opened to the public at ten, and she got there a few minutes early to turn lights on and empty the overnight drop box. The Monday-morning box always held the most books since the library was closed on Sundays. She spread them out on the desk by genre and found the most popular category was thriller/mystery. Of course it was!

The library had a few volunteers in addition to Rebecca being the full-time librarian. Today, Mary was stopping in for a few hours mid-day. She had the quintessential head of tight grey curls that came with her age. While Rebecca had never asked, she was guessing that Mary was an octogenarian. "What can I do for you today, sweetie?" Mary enjoyed Rebecca's company, and Rebecca enjoyed being able to chat with someone who had seen so much in her lifetime.

"Mary, this day is going by so slowly, I figured you weren't coming in."

"Dear, I'm right on time, as always." Mary was right, as always. She arrived at noon, just as planned, just as she did every Monday. "Need any help in the office or maybe putting away books from this morning?"

"I finished the books from the drop box, but I have several books on reserve that arrived today from other libraries that need calling. Would you mind?"

"No problem, dear. Just show me the list, and I'll get right to it." Mary settled into a chair at the desk behind the marble check-out counter. "Love your shirt, by the way. Very cute."

Rebecca was known for her collection of book-themed shirts. Today she was wearing one in a very noticeable font that read, 'Librarian because Book Wizard isn't an Official Job Title.' She was confident that Mary didn't understand the connection, but much like Harry, Rebecca often felt like a wizard with untapped skills.

"Mary, do you mind if I run home quickly to turn on my crockpot about 1pm?"

"I'm sure I'll be done with these calls by then. Of course you can run home."

"Thanks." Rebecca checked the clock again... 12:04pm. "I'll just be in the children's section setting up the new end cap until then. Holler if you need me."

"Can do." Mary set to highlighting the lists of names and numbers to make the calls easier while Rebecca disappeared into the children's section. She picked out books at a variety of reading levels about gardening and farming. She'd been thinking about all of the fresh vegetables and fruits on their way to New Hampshire this summer, and she just had to share her joy. The display was almost finished when Mary popped her head around the corner.

"Didn't you say you wanted to head home at one?"

"Oh no, am I late?"

"No, dear. It's 12:55pm, so I figured I'd come and let you know."

For the first time today, Rebecca had become distracted by something she loved more than solving a mystery, and that was her love of reading. She gathered her keys and practical handbag and waved to Mary on her way out. "Thanks again. See you in a few." Rebecca's house was only a few blocks away, so it was a quick trip.

Rebecca walked through the front doorway after unlocking both the door and deadbolt – couldn't be too safe. She walked straight back to the kitchen, past the exposed staircase on her right that went to the second

18

floor. Joey and Bean got a few moments of attention each and topped-off bowls of dry food. She had taken out the crockpot this morning and laid out all of the ingredients to make this go as quickly as possible. Canned tomatoes and tomato paste joined a variety of spices in the small pot; it was a basic design she had picked up on sale the day after Christmas, but it got the job done.

Remembering that Kenny didn't like chunks in his sauce, she took out the immersion blender and remedied the potential situation. He had originally been too polite to tell her that he liked a smooth sauce. She caught him sliding the biggest tomato chunks to the edge of his pasta bowl one night when he was over for dinner. Ever since, she had blended the sauce on nights he joined her. The meatballs she made this morning had been placed in the refrigerator to wait – into the sauce they went. She covered the pot and turned it on low before carefully racing back to the library.

The rest of the shift crawled along. Mary was only there for a few hours and waved goodbye as she headed home. Her hours at the library kept her young, she professed, and Rebecca agreed. At 5:55pm the library was ready to be locked up. Rebecca was known for staying open an extra few minutes most nights, but tonight she was walking to her car as the clock on her phone switched to 6pm.

Headlights shown through the front bay window at five minutes to seven. She had plenty of time to make small side salads and get the pasta water ready. When Kenny got to the door, he entered without knocking, just like Rebecca had recommended the last ten times he had come over for dinner. "Hey there!" she called out from the kitchen. Not wanting to seem too eager, she forced herself to wait there while the final minutes passed. "What did you bring me?"

"Information...or would you rather the raspberry iced tea I'm carrying?" Kenny did his best to show his appreciation for her efforts to be there for him.

"Ummm, both. Can I say both?"

"Sure you can, but only once I've got some of your amazing meatballs in my belly."

"Sorry I couldn't make fresh pasta. Just didn't happen with the work schedule tonight. Maybe next time."

"It's a date." Kenny started to blush and looked at his feet. He nervously shuffled toward the fridge where he placed the single bottle of tea inside the shelf on the door. "You know what I mean."

Rebecca dropped the capellini into the water. It was perfect with the blended sauce as it was somewhere between spaghetti and angel hair pasta. Kenny wasn't too picky, but this would be ready quickly so they could get to talking. She had places already set at the island in the kitchen. The formal dining room was dark as she rarely used it. "Anything interesting happen lately for you?" She tried to move the conversation away from the awkward 'date' comment.

"You could say that." He walked over to the island and sat down in his seat. He had a seat.

It made Rebecca smile to think that he had his own seat, well, stool. "Any preference on salad dressing?"

He looked at her with one raised eyebrow. "Has my answer ever changed?"

"No, but I'm hoping some day it might." She retrieved his bottle of creamy ranch from the fridge. "How can you eat this stuff?"

"Been eating it since I was a kid. Why stop now?"

"Your health, for one." Rebecca tried not to mother him, but he made it too easy. The pasta was ready to drain so she used a colander and plated both of their meals. "So, what can you tell me, and what do I need to drag out of you with a bribe of a homemade dessert?"

"I'm pretty sure I'd give you all of my passwords to just about everything if you made strawberry shortcake. You did make strawberry shortcake, didn't you?"

"We'll see. Spill it." She slid two large bowls of pasta with sauce and meatballs across the island. Kenny's favorite part was how she cooked the meatballs in the crockpot, so they weren't hard or crispy on the outside. One might call him a picky eater.

"Next of kin was notified, so it'll be in The Record tomorrow. I hate to tell you, but it was Max."

"Max? Like, the Joseph Maxfield we went to high school with...that Max?"

"Yep. Been back here, what, two years?"

"Geeze. About that I'd say." Rebecca hadn't been close to Max in high school or since he'd been back in the area, but it was someone she'd know most of her life. "What happened?"

"We're not sure yet. We're waiting on information about whether he was dead before he went into the water or if he drowned." At this, Rebecca shivered. "We don't have to talk about it. We can just enjoy this amazing dinner you made."

"No, I want to help in any way I can, and I do love a good mystery. This just hits a little closer to home than the books I read from the library. Any leads?"

"I'm not sure leads is the right word. Everyone liked Max. He bartended at The Catch of the Day in the summer but since he'd been back, he was working at the hardware store too. Really can't find anyone to say a bad word about him."

"Do you think it's related to either job or something personal?"

"Well, the first lead was an argument at the bar Saturday night. Things got heated with Donny after a few too many drinks."

Rebecca rolled her eyes. This was not surprising by any means, and it certainly wasn't the first time Donny got loud in public where alcohol was involved. "Why would that make him a suspect or person of interest?"

Kenny moaned as he chewed a mouthful of pasta, sauce and meatball. "Everything about this is divine. Thank you for having me over for dinner, even if it was to get me to talk." He smiled and paused while he watched Rebecca wipe sauce from her lip. She missed a small spot on her chin, and he reached over to get it for her. "Sorry. Habit." Kenny had two adorable children. He was all too familiar with messy sauce cleanup on pasta nights, but his sauce came out of a glass jar. At least he made dinners, and they included vegetables – double points.

"Well, the fact that he yelled, 'I'd kill to get another drink right now,' didn't help prove his innocence. Donny was angry Max had cut him off, and he figured maybe yelling would help get him another drink. It didn't, and he spent quite a while trying to convince Ben to get him one more when Max wasn't looking. Ben, of course, called a ride for Donny."

"Any other suspects?" Rebecca was happy to move this along while she enjoyed her dinner. "Oh, I forgot the iced tea you brought me." She hopped up and grabbed it from the door of the fridge. Her favorite brand even – more bonus points. "What do you want to drink?"

"Just a glass of water, thanks. So, the last person to see Max alive was Ben. Doesn't mean he's a person of interest, but if you're the last person to see someone alive, that is always *of interest*."

"I mean, we've known Ben our whole lives. What motive could he possibly have?"

"Don't know, but Max is dead, and there are no solid leads."

"So, is that it?"

Kenny played with his pasta and slowly chewed a small bite.

"Is there something you want to tell me but feel you can't?" Rebecca could read him well by now.

"Hmmm. So, I'm not sure this is public knowledge. Max had a significant other."

"Really?!" How did she not know? Gossip flowed freely around the lake, especially as it got warmer and gathering places like The Catch of the Day opened back up. "Who?"

"Someone he grew up with."

Rebecca pondered this one. She took a few bites of her dry salad with no croutons. She felt this balanced all of the carbs in the pasta. It didn't, but it made her feel like she was making an effort to walk the walk when she just hounded Kenny about his ranch dressing. She tried to stare him down.

"They might even work together," Kenny confessed.

"Molly? No way. They are nothing alike."

"Didn't hear it from me." Kenny winked then looked down at his empty pasta bowl, appearing to decide if he should at least have a few bites of salad since she had gone out of her way to make it.

"No, I didn't, but why would a significant other be a suspect?" Rebecca watched to see if Kenny was going to touch the salad with ranch.

"She believes she was the last person to see him alive and appears to feel really guilty about it. Don't know, but it's a gut feeling, so I'm not crossing her off the list. The other piece of information that makes things a little curious is that it appears they were keeping things secret. No one else seemed to know they were an item." They exchanged silent but quizzical looks.

"So, if I did make strawberry shortcake – with home-made biscuits – would you have any other suspects on your short list?"

"If I say no, do I lose out on the shortcake?"

"I made it for you, so I suppose you get it no matter what." Relief spread over Kenny's face.

"We don't have any other suspects or people of interest, and that's unnerving. We'd love to have a lead that seems strong, but we just don't. We will look at everything with fresh eyes in the morning and hope for some information about cause of death."

"Are we full enough to start a movie, or are you going to head out as soon as you get dessert?"

"Depends on what movie you are offering. If it's Titanic, I need to get my dessert to go. If we're talking something like Goonies or Back to the Future, I'm in."

"Chief's choice." Rebecca made her way to the freezer to pull out the metal bowl and beaters. "Good thing you're staying, 'cause I wasn't going to make the whipped cream otherwise."

"Can I help?" Kenny always offered, even though Rebecca rarely took him up on it.

"Could you put wet food in the cat bowls then get the movie cued up? I'll be in with dessert in a few. Do you want lots of juice or dry biscuits?"

"Is there a right answer?" He opened the two containers of wet food that had been waiting on the counter while attempting to not step on tails or pour the food on either head.

"Yes," Rebecca responded, not telling him which was right.

"I'll take it that way." After quickly disposing of the containers and washing his hands, he left the kitchen with a grin.

Rebecca finally had a chance to think alone for the first time tonight. Donny, Ben and Molly. Was that really the best the police had come up with? It's a good thing she was on the case as well, behind the scenes at least. She decided that an early lunch was her best plan for tomorrow since the library didn't open until 1pm on Tuesdays. She split the biscuits in half and placed them flat in the bottom of two clean pasta bowls. She whipped up some homemade whipped cream. Just before turning on the electric hand mixer, she heard Kenny on his phone in the living room saying goodnight to his children. How he ended up divorced she'd never understand.

Full ladles of strawberries with lots of juice were poured over the biscuits then topped with heaping scoops of whipped cream. She carried the bowls, with spoons, into the living room where Kenny had picked Ferris Bueller's Day Off. They sat and ate in companionable silence while they watched the classic from their childhood, occasionally quoting lines.

When Kenny got up to leave, Rebecca stopped him. "Wait. I have your lunch for tomorrow." She had thoughtfully made extras for him to warm up. The Tupperware was waiting in the fridge where she placed it before making the whipped cream. Returning to the living room, she handed him the dish, large enough for two servings. "Just wanted to make sure you ate something. You know, in case the day was especially long."

They looked at each other for a beat longer than expected and almost dropped the container when she broke the moment backing up.

"Thanks for this. I really appreciate it." Kenny's voice broke slightly. "Dinner and dessert were perfect."

"Be careful, and I hope you get some new information about the cause of death tomorrow. Still can't believe it was Max."

"We'll do our best. Have a good day at work." And with that, he left via the door he had entered almost three hours ago.

Rebecca returned to the kitchen with the discarded dessert bowls and cleaned up before heading to bed. She considered writing down all of the questions she had for Ben, but her eyes were just too tired. After a trip to the bathroom, she landed on her bed, falling asleep almost instantly.

# Chapter 4

## *The Owner*

While The Catch of the Day didn't open until 11am, Rebecca pulled into the parking lot at 10:45am. She was just as impatient to get started as she had been the day before. Kenny said that Ben was only a suspect because he was the last person to see Max alive, but she planned to find out if that was really the whole story. She walked up to the employee entrance at the back of the restaurant and knocked after having already checked for Ben's SUV.

As luck would have it, Ben poked his head out of the door and smiled. "Rebecca, what's dragged you out so early?" He silently read her shirt, moving his lips with each word as he did. 'It's A Good Day To Read A Book.' "You normally show up a little later on Tuesdays." He was right. While Tuesday was the one weekday that the library opened late enough to enjoy a lakeside lunch, she usually showed up at half past eleven or so.

"Wanted to see how you were doing."

"Why?" Ben looked genuinely confused by the statement.

She paused. "Well, because your bartender, and childhood friend, was just pulled out of the lake on Sunday, deceased. I figured you might be a bit shook up." She watched him intently. His look of confusion quickly shifting to one of concern, even sadness.

"Yeah. Well, it's been all-hands-on-deck to cover, so I really haven't had time to think about it much."

"Want to sit down and talk about it for a few?" Rebecca had always been a gentle soul and very kind-hearted. It wasn't out of character for her to look out for her former classmates and friends like this, even if this time she had an ulterior motive.

"Sure. Let's sit at the bar. Kitchen's not ready yet, but want a drink?"

"Kinda early, so a virgin strawberry daiquiri sounds good. It has fruit in it, so that counts for breakfast, right?" At least *she* thought she was funny. Ben walked around to the back side of the bar and Rebecca took a seat on one of the stools. "Know anything about what happened with Max?"

"Nope. We stayed late Saturday night after closing, shared some whiskey and when it was time to leave, he was already gone. Never said good night because he's got his own keys, and I thought we were both closing up. When I stopped back at the bar, the place was empty." The sound of the blender stopped their conversation for a moment.

"As far as Saturday nights go, how was the shift?" Ben

passed her the drink in a real glass. Most of the time her drinks came in tall Styrofoam cups.

"Max was here from open to close. Saturdays are busy, and tips can be great, so he always works them...I mean, worked them." Ben looked sad, like he was processing what he just said, but Rebecca couldn't be sure if it was genuine or for her sake.

"So, it was a good night?"

"Well, he had a strange interaction with Donny. Remember Donny from school?"

"Of course. I was in kindergarten with Donny. I didn't hang out with him outside of school, but we were always friendly. What was the interaction?" She sipped her drink.

"I didn't see it, only heard the end of it. Donny seemed pretty drunk and yelled, 'I'd kill to get another drink right about now.' I stepped in and walked him out back to get a ride home. I called and paid for it. Wasn't too late, maybe ten."

Well, at least that was consistent. Kenny had the same information, and that was good news for Ben. When things didn't match up, it caused people to wonder.

"Anything else about Saturday that involved Max?"

"Nothing I can think of. I don't want to be rude, but I've got to get ready to open. Want me to put in a lunch order for you as soon as the kitchen is ready?"

"Why don't I help. Is there anything I could do to make the opening easier?"

"If you're serious, it would be great if you could check

the center of the tables and restock the buckets." The tables all had small metal pails in the middle with menus, napkins, plastic utensils, salt and pepper shakers, etc. It was a sit-down restaurant but a casual one. The beach was literally across the one-way street, so the pails were a cute addition to the lakeside charm.

"Happy to help since it means I get priority seating." She winked but was serious at the same time. She had a preferred table she rarely got to sit at on Tuesday mornings.

"You've got it. Set your drink down and let me know what you want me to order for you."

Rebecca dropped off her half-full daiquiri glass and picked up a menu. Why she picked up a menu she didn't know. The offerings rarely changed, so she knew what she wanted already. "Fried clam basket – whole bellies – with french fries." She had to holler since she had walked away.

"Got it. Thanks for the help."

She bustled around and quickly checked all of the pails and refilled what needed refilling. Once finished, she sat at her table with the car-free front-row view of the lake and peacefully enjoyed her drink. The sky was threatening, but no rain currently, and the awning wasn't out yet. The clouds meant she didn't need sunscreen or a hat to protect her fair skin – small miracles.

"Here you go. One basket of fried – whole belly – clams with french fries and tarter sauce on the side." This time it was Ben who winked.

"Hey, it's not busy yet. Sit with me so we can talk about Max for a bit."

Ben checked his surroundings. Things were quiet and the weather, coupled with the day of the week, meant it was probably going to be a slow lunch service. "Sure. Let me grab my drink."

He returned with a glass of water. "What did you want to talk about?"

"Remember that time in elementary school when Max was glued to his seat? No one ever did confess."

"No, they didn't. Max was mortified being carried out of the class by two custodians while still sitting in the chair." Ben relaxed back in the seat. It was the first time Rebecca saw anything that looked like he was letting his guard down. "Do you remember the time Max was taken by ambulance in, what was it, fourth grade?"

"Sure do. Right after lunch. It was a Friday too, so we didn't know what happened until Monday. Ah, the easier times without cell phones and email." Having grown up as Xennials – on the cusp of Gen-X and Millennials – Ben and Rebecca really did remember and miss the slower, easier times.

"He had some kind of allergic reaction, but not a big one. If I remember correctly, the nurse wasn't there that day, so they had to call for the ambulance."

"Oh, and the time in high school when they figured out he had alcohol intolerance – not an allergy – but beer was off the menu after that."

"It's funny that all of our memories of Max are semi-traumatic."

"That's why we remember them. Who remembers the time Max drove safely to school? No one."

They shared space at the table while Rebecca finished up her fried lunch, and Ben just sipped his drink as he stared out at the mountains. "Well, guess I should get up and help. Tables are filling up, and the bar won't serve itself."

"So, you're filling in at the bar since Max is...gone?"

"No choice. I'm asking around at other places in the area, but who wants to give up a year-round job for something that lasts three or four months?"

"I hope you find some help. You'll burn out if you have to do it all yourself for the whole summer."

"Keep an ear to the ground for me, and send me any leads on a potential bartender. I may have to resort to asking Sara...ugh." Sara was Ben's younger, less responsible, sister who lived above the restaurant. She couldn't seem to hold down a consistent job, and Ben already had a place to live when he built the restaurant. He felt like looking after her was his responsibility, so he let her live there, practically rent free. At least if he did hire Sara, temporarily, she couldn't blame her car breaking down on being late to work.

"Will do. Want me to leave the money on the table or hand it to you since you were my server today?"

"On the house. Thanks for helping me get set up."

"Well, I'll leave a good tip. Thanks." Rebecca got up and bussed her own table, a helper through and through. As she walked to the ice cream window, she considered if there was anything else she should have asked Ben when she had him to herself. It really felt like without more information from Kenny, she couldn't have done more.

"Small chocolate chip cookie dough in a dish, please."

"Coming right up." The teenager inside the ice cream window walked back to the chest freezers to scoop the ice cream into a Styrofoam bowl. "Anything else?"

"That's all. Thanks." Rebecca handed her a five-dollar bill then accepted her change, dropping it in the tip cup, and walked along the edge of the beach, careful not to get sand in her work shoes.

The sound of the water lapping the shore was peaceful, but she was deep in thought about what to do next. Would Donny or Molly be the next stop for questioning? Since Molly hadn't been at The Catch of the Day when she left, it didn't make sense to try to talk to her. Showing up at her house or calling would be out of character, so a quick stop at Donny's gift shop, The Lakehouse, seemed like the next logical step before work at two. She turned around and walked back to her car, dropping her small bowl and spoon in the recycling bin on the way by the corner of the restaurant. She checked the clock on the dash. She figured she had about thirty minutes to devote to The Lakehouse before she would need to hustle off to the library. "Better get going," she said to herself.

# Chapter 5

## *The Inebriated*

Nine identical notes from a single bell rang above the door to the not-so-small gift shop located in town. Though it was not near the lake, it was called The Lakehouse and had been an ever-expanding location to pick up tacky sweatshirts and exquisite handmade artifacts from local artists in equal measure for decades. The rotating rack of screen-printed tops stood at the right, directly below a wall covered in gorgeous paintings of sunsets and sunrises from all over Newfound Lake. To the left was a counter, built well over fifty years ago, that had seen thousands of sales and dozens of different cash registers. Next to the current cash register sat a cell phone with one of those devices to swipe a credit card. While the cell phone service in and around town was questionable, here at The Lakehouse it worked well enough to pay your bill digitally.

"Good afternoon," came a gruff voice from behind

the counter. Up popped the head and slowly the body of Donny, the next person of interest.

"Good afternoon to you too."

"Rebecca, haven't seen you in here in a while." It wasn't really a question or a statement, just a neutral observation. The two had known each other since they were young but were never close friends. Occasionally, Rebecca stopped in to pick up something as a gift for visiting friends or family, but it was rarely for herself.

"Well, I decided that I wanted to put together a gift basket for a friend, and this seemed like the best place to get everything I needed in one spot." She was right. Beautiful handwoven baskets hung from ceiling hooks above her head. When she decided on the perfect one for her 'gift,' she reached for it, only to find out she was about two inches too short. "Donny, do you have a step stool around here I might use?"

"I'll get it for you." He brought the step stool because he wasn't any taller than Rebecca. At about five foot six inches, that made her height average and his below average. It took a few moments for him to get there and up to the right step. "This one?"

"Next one over, please. The darker one. Thanks." This was going to be an expensive reconnaissance mission, but she would figure out who to give the basket to eventually. "Do you know who makes these?"

"Sure do. Mrs. Josephson, up on Slate Hill Road. She's been selling them here longer than I can remember."

"Great. Just wanted to make sure it was local. Always

try to support local." Rebecca really wasn't prepared for how to handle this visit. She needed to figure out a way to get around to talking about Saturday night, but since she only just left The Catch of the Day a few minutes ago and decided on a whim to sneak this in before going to work, her plan was not very well thought out. "You sell mostly local, right?"

"Of course. Doesn't make sense in this economy to ship things in, even if it wasn't just the right thing to do. Selling local, I mean. Gotta think about the bottom line too." Donny sounded much older than his chronological age.

"I feel the same way about shopping here. I'm sure I could order a basket of New Hampshire items online, but I feel better patronizing your business." Her grin was ear to ear as she tried to butter him up, but there was no amount of butter that was going to cover up his burnt-toast mood today.

"Do you have a specific room or location for food items?" The Lakehouse had once been a home, a very long time ago. She was standing in what she believed to be the original living room. There was a staircase that led up to what were once bedrooms, and every room seemed to now have a theme.

"Top of the stairs on the right." He was facing the wall behind the counter now, putting away the step stool, so he shouted over his shoulder.

"Thanks." She ascended the stairs two steps at a time. She didn't really need any of this, but what she did need was an excuse to be in the store. In the former bedroom at the top of the stairs, she quickly gathered local honey, dried herbs, maple syrup, maple candies and a few jars of jam. Returning to the first floor, she slowly made her way to the counter to pay. Paying meant she was done and needed to leave, but she couldn't leave yet.

Her eyes started to search the counter where they landed on a stack of newspapers. This small town still had a newspaper, The Record, and the headline was now her saving grace. "Did you see the paper this morning?" she inquired innocently.

Donny turned around. "How could I miss it? I was there." He looked down at the items she had gathered, completely unphased by the news he had just volunteered. Rebecca, on the other hand, had to contain her excitement. Not only had the paper given her the necessary segue to talk about Max's death, but Donny just admitted to having been there. Was that a slip of the tongue? She examined his face, but it gave nothing away – he was all business.

"What do you mean, you were there? When did you see him last?"

"When I was being kindly escorted out of the restaurant by Ben. Pretty sure I didn't deserve my premature exit from the evening, but there it was."

"Why were you escorted out?" She already knew a little bit from Kenny, but any first-hand information was better than second or third. "Was Max still there when you left?"

"Sure was. He was the reason I got kicked out, and after I bought him a drink too. Ingrate."

"Why would you buy Max a drink?"

"That waitress he'd been seeing, she yelled at him, and I felt bad. I was drinking alone, and he seemed pretty miserable, so I figured I'd buy him a shot of whiskey to cheer him up."

"Did he drink the shot?" Rebecca remembered he had alcohol intolerance, so it didn't make sense he would even accept the shot, let alone drink it. She'd have to ask questions about the waitress, presumably Molly, after.

"I offered him a beer first, and he said he couldn't drink beer. I asked if it was because he was on the clock, and he said it would make him sick, but he would share a shot of whiskey with me, so we did."

"Wow. Didn't know he could drink alcohol at all." Rebecca made a mental note of this to tell Kenny. She didn't think he knew about this detail. "Don't you remember in high school when he found out he had a problem with alcohol?"

"No recollection of that. He had a sip of the shot before that waitress came over and yelled at him again. Jokes on him. He left the shot there so later, when Ben kicked me out, I downed the shot before he could *remove* me."

"What waitress came over and yelled at him? What did she say?"

"She said, 'Why don't you go home with her instead!' I turned to see what was happening, and Max was serving a girl at the end of the bar. I didn't see or hear anything specific, but the waitress sure was upset."

"Do you remember which waitress? Was it someone

new for the summer?" Rebecca realized she was a little too excited in her delivery, reminding herself to stay calm.

"No. That girl we went to high school with who works at The Catch of the Day and works at the diner in town year-round too."

"Molly?"

"Yeah, Molly."

Well, this was quite the turn of events. Rebecca finally had a statement supporting the notion that Max was involved with Molly, and now there was a reason to want to interview her for more than just thinking she was the last one to see Max alive. Kenny didn't officially tell her about the relationship, so it was going to be tricky figuring out what to say, but this was handed to her on a silver platter.

"What happened when she yelled at him?"

"Don't know for sure. Bar was pretty busy, and she walked away. He was stuck behind the bar on a Saturday night. Shortly after, I got kicked out for 'making a threat' that wasn't really a threat."

"You made a threat?"

"Max was at the other end of the bar for a while, so I yelled, 'I'd kill for another drink.' Max didn't find it funny and called Ben over to remove me. That's when I drank his shot. No harm, no foul. I wasn't going to actually kill anyone, but they decided I'd had too many drinks. Ben sent me home in a car...not sure whose at this point. I don't remember anything else. I woke up Sunday morning and came to work. Opened the shop late too."

"So, you never saw anyone else that night?" She did

not do a very good job of staying calm, even after trying to reel herself in.

"Why do you ask?"

"Oh, nothing. Just that I was at The Catch of the Day when they recovered Max's body, and I just can't stop thinking about all of it. Trying to make things make sense in my head. So terrible."

"Yeah. Terrible. Well, total is $159." Donny clearly did not feel the same way about Max's death.

"That's more than I expected, but ok. Shopping local isn't always cheap, but you won't regret it. My mom always said if you pay for the best, you'll never be disappointed."

"Sounds like a smart woman. Always loved your mother."

"Thanks. Off to work. Maybe I'll see you around this summer."

"Maybe, if they let me back at the bar. Have a good day." Donny nodded and returned to whatever he had been doing below the counter.

"You too." With that, Rebecca walked back out the front door of the store – nine chimes of the bell sounding her exit. She strode to her car, dropping the basket of goodies on the front passenger seat and taking her spot on the other side of the car. One hundred fifty-nine dollars was a lot for her wallet, but she felt she got some good information from Donny, and not a whiff of sadness nor dishonesty. That was worth every penny. She'd find somewhere for the gift basket to go, even if it wasn't until Christmas. Putting the car in reverse, she backed out of the spot along the side of the building. She pulled onto the road, placing the car into drive and noticed the clock on the dash. "Oh no!" She realized she had four minutes to get the library opened. On the only day they opened late all week, the return box would be full, and she would start the day at a disadvantage. With no Mary expected today, she was in for a marathon and a sprint, all at the same time.

# Chapter 6

## *The Library*

WITH AN EXTRA HOP IN HER STEP, REBECCA KEYED into the library at 1:01pm. She entered from the basement to turn off the alarm then ran up the stairs to street level. She opened the front door after taking in a deep breath. No one was standing there waiting to be let in as she appreciated the smell that only a whole building of library books had. Not that the library patrons tended to be too feisty, but it was the only day they opened in the afternoon. The person who ran an after-school activity on Tuesdays would be here soon to set up, so she knew she needed to get moving. After grabbing the books from the overnight drop box, she closed the front door behind her with her foot and dropped the stack on the counter. She walked around the counter and carefully placed the books into groups before realizing the lights weren't even on in most of the library.

Funding for the property, building and initial collection of books had been donated by two men who had grown up in town and made a name for themselves individually in the late 1800s. The building was an amazing work of structural art and had been well maintained over the years. Rebecca was proud to be the current steward. She was born and raised around Newfound Lake; many houses in the area had been her home for various periods of time. She moved away for college but came back because she knew this was where she belonged. Many members of the community never left because they didn't feel they had the ability to, but she returned because it was home.

Immediately upon confirming all lights were on, Karen arrived to set up for the after-school activity. This week she was planning to read *The Book With No Pictures* and then challenge the children to make a book with no words. She carried in milk crates of supplies so the kids could use a multitude of mixed media in their creations. She wholeheartedly believed that kids didn't get enough opportunities to be kids and create without boundaries – she did recognize that creating a book with no words was a restriction. Both Rebecca and Karen knew it would result in a disaster in the children's section but a worthwhile one.

"Afternoon!" The tone of her voice said she was having a good day, so Rebecca smiled.

"I do hope it is going to be a good afternoon. Do you have many kiddos signed up for today?"

Karen dropped her current load of supplies and returned to the check-out desk. "Ten right now, but there could always be drop-ins." Her boxy capris, linen shirt and oversized cardigan made her look older than she was, but the sandy-brown wavy cut that stopped just above the shoulder gave away her true personality.

"How you wrangle ten kids under ten at the same time, I'll never know."

Karen was an elementary school art teacher turned children's book author. She illustrated her own books, so she was a one-woman show. She offered the after-school activities to give back to the community since she was no longer a full-time teacher. "Ten is nothing after you've had twenty-one under six. Plus, I miss the kids." She hadn't found her special someone yet so there were no kids at home to fill that current void. At twenty-five, she still had plenty of time for that.

The door opened to the library, and Rebecca looked up to welcome whoever was crossing the threshold. Much to her surprise, Kenny entered in full uniform. "To what do we owe this surprise visit, Chief Towne?" Rebecca greeted. Karen looked at Rebecca, then the chief, then back at Rebecca. Since neither of them were looking at her, she faded off into the children's section to continue preparing the afternoon activity.

"Looks like I am following in your footsteps today. Just stopped by The Lakehouse after visiting The Catch of the Day, and both Donny and Ben said they had just seen you. Anything I should know about, Rebecca?" It was a loaded question. She knew he knew the answer but wanted her to know he knew she was taking on her own investigation, so to speak.

"Ummm, nothing in particular. I needed lunch

before work, and I had a gift to purchase." Her cheeks began to turn a light shade of pink, easily visible against her naturally pale skin.

"Funny. Both men said that you spoke with them, at length, about a recently deceased classmate."

"Well, it is on the front page of the paper at The Lakehouse, and I was at the restaurant when his body was recovered. I'm sure it makes sense why the conversation turned that way." The light shade of pink looked more like a purposeful makeup choice, but she was not going to break. "Chief Towne, were you at both of those places today speaking with both of those men about the same recently deceased classmate?"

"I'm not going to confirm or deny that, but you need to be a little less forward with your meddlesome tendencies."

"Chief Towne, I would never..."

"Yeah, yeah, Rebecca. Anyway, looks like..." Chief Towne looked in the direction of Karen then back to Rebecca and whispered, "This does not appear to be an accident." Rebecca inhaled sharply and also glanced in the direction of Karen. No change, so they both continued with the conversation as if he had not just revealed something groundbreaking. Back at full volume, he asked, "Want me to bring over pizza some night this week?"

"Hmmm...only if it comes with a side of fried pickles."

"Who has fried pickles in town?" His arms rose and fell with the question.

"Not sure, but don't show up without them. Let me know when you plan to come over."

Chief Towne turned to leave and said over his shoulder at a raised volume, "Have a nice day, Karen."

Karen popped her head around a corner to wave. "Oh, you too, Chief Towne."

"See you soon, Ms. Ramsey."

As the door closed behind him, Karen ran to the window to make sure he had left for good. "That man has it bad for you."

"No, he doesn't. We are perfect friends. We enjoy each other's company and require nothing more from the other person than that. He has an ex and kids that take up most of his time, and I have the library and my cats."

"A woman cannot rely on cats alone. He's offering to bring over pizza...to your house."

"We've had plenty of nights like that since his divorce, and it's purely platonic."

"If he shows up with the fried pickles, you'll know they are *not* platonic intentions on his part."

"It's just pizza and a chance to talk about what happened to Max. You heard, right?" This was Rebecca's way of checking that the whisper shared by Chief Towne was still a secret.

"It's tragic. I read the paper, but there doesn't seem to be any real information yet. No one knows, or is saying, if he died of an accident, natural causes or homicide. What could Chief Towne possibly need to talk to you about... over pizza and fried pickles?"

"Well, he may have been right that I was talking to

two people this morning before work, but it was only to confirm that they are innocent and that I shouldn't be worried about it being anything nefarious."

"Aaannnnd, did you confirm that it was nothing nefarious?"

"I confirmed nothing and only added to my list of unknowns. That is why I accepted the pizza invitation."

"Date is more like it." Karen removed the cardigan and draped it over the back of a small chair meant for the children.

"It is not a date." Date. There was that word again. Rebecca did not think it was a date. She was confident that Chief Towne did not think of it as a date either. It was simply pizza, and hopefully fried pickles, and a lot of discussion about what they both knew regarding the death of a high school friend.

And Max was a friend. He wasn't the type of friend you hung out with every weekend, but when you sat down at his bar, you felt like he knew everything about you and you about him. He was a peaceful soul who just wanted to relax by the lake and earn enough to get by at the same time. His loss really was devastating, and not just as a headline.

"Well, the kids will be here soon, and I need to be prepared. You can stand there and think about your not-date while you work."

"I will...not."

Rebecca finished her otherwise uneventful shift that night and went home to spend time with her cats, her mind reeling with this new detail – not an accident. She did feel a little guilty that she left her house so early on a night she worked late. Tuesdays were always tough on them, and they required extra loves when she got home. She rubbed bellies and talked in a voice higher than expected for her, all while sitting just inside the front door. "What were you two doing while I was working all day?" They rolled and purred uncontrollably. Rebecca knew she had the two best kitties in the world. Joey and Bean were her everything. "I can't believe you two let me go this long without demanding wet food."

Wet food was supplied, as it was every night, just a little later because it was Tuesday. While they ate, she decided she wasn't going to have dinner tonight – one small blessing of living alone. She went upstairs, got ready for bed and watched the first ten minutes of a cooking competition show before falling asleep on top of the covers. While she slept, she dreamed of a successful discussion with Molly, though she was unsure what 'successful' meant in this context.

# Chapter 7

## *The Waitress*

Rebecca had a full day of work at the library ahead of her to prepare what she wanted to say when she got to The Catch of the Day. She couldn't be sure but hoped Molly would be working; that was a variable out of her control. The second unknown was how busy the restaurant would be. If they were slammed, she wouldn't be able to chat at all. "What are we going to do today?" she cooed to Joey and Bean. They did figure-eights through her legs when she reached the bottom of the stairs. "I may be out late again tonight, so I should treat you to an extra special breakfast." Rebecca strode to the cabinet to get containers of wet food. She didn't often give them treats, and wet food in the morning was a treat, but she was feeling pretty guilty about how much she was gone already this week. Bean practically climbed up her legs as she walked over to the food dishes. "Well, you two will have to play nice while I am out." The two cats happily devoured their treats while

Rebecca packed up a lunch and made her way out the front door.

She piled her bag, lunch and laptop onto the front seat of the green Subaru. The trusty hatchback wasn't going to catch anyone's attention, but it didn't come with a car payment and was reliable in the winter; the latter was much more important. She drove to the library where she loaded everything back into her arms before approaching the door to enter. Balancing it all in one arm now, she unlocked the front door and closed it behind her with her foot. The bag and laptop were deposited on the curved check-out desk while she wandered into the office to store her lunch in the mini fridge. In her haste to leave last night, it appeared that she had left the office computer on. That lack of attention to detail was not like her. Clearly, this *investigation* was distracting her from real responsibilities. The death of her high school friend would be taken care of by the police, including her current and close friend Kenny. She couldn't allow herself to give less than her best to her actual job.

The time passed slowly, and she checked her phone repeatedly to see if anyone, Kenny especially, might text her with new information or at least a projected date for pizza – not-date for pizza. No texts and very few patrons made for another long shift. Rebecca decided to change the end cap near the front door to feature mystery authors. Agatha Christie was an obvious choice, but she spent a long time adding books by Dan Brown, Louise Penny, John Grisham, P.D. James, Thomas Harris and Stieg Larsson. When she chose which books to feature, she looked for the book that had been taken out the fewest times by each author and placed it next to the book the author was most famous for. She didn't know if there was an actual science to getting readers to explore new authors or lesser-known titles by famous authors, but this seemed as good an idea as any.

When she next looked at a clock, it was already past six. "Where has the time gone?" She quickly packed up her things, leaving the lunch in the fridge as she never remembered to eat it earlier. She'd be back tomorrow, and that meant one less thing to remember in the morning. The green Subaru was waiting in the parking lot, all alone, for her to drive back out to the foot of the lake for dinner. It was good that Kenny hadn't tried to get together tonight because she would be one person-of-interest short for her not-date over pizza.

The parking lot was packed already. The Catch of the Day was *the* place to go when the weather was good, and tonight was a magical night to eat out on the deck. Sunset was still a bit off, and Rebecca hated to take up a whole table by herself. She walked in and took a single stool at the bar. A woman she recognized immediately was stocking glasses. When their eyes met, both women broke into easy smiles.

"Rebecca, how are you? Crazy around here, huh?" Sara, Ben's little sister, was indeed behind the bar.

"Well, fancy seeing you here. I just spoke to Ben yesterday about hiring a bartender, and you're already filling the position."

"Not like he gave me much of a choice. 'Sara, if

you're going to live here virtually rent free, the least you can do is pitch in and help.'" Sara mocked Ben's business-like tone and straightened her imaginary tie in the process. "I would not, however, advise ordering any mixed drinks if you know how they should taste. So, what can I get you?"

Rebecca hadn't thought about an answer yet, but she knew she was starving. When she was busy at the library, she wasn't thinking about food, but now she felt like she could eat half the fish in Newfound. "Can I put in an order for a calamari appetizer while I think about what else I want?"

"Spicy mayo or marinara?" Sara looked up from the small notepad she was writing on.

"Oh, marinara, please."

"Sure. Something easy to drink?"

"Root beer, please."

"No problem." Sara winked and wandered off, presumably to put in the order for the calamari. Luckily for Sara, she looked nothing like her brother. Where he was stalky, she was wiry. Where he had thick, dark hair, she had shoulder-length, wispy blonde hair. Really, they hardly looked related. When she returned, she poured the root beer and then walked to the other end of the bar. "We'll catch up more later," she called out over the noises in the active watering hole.

"Molly!" Rebecca shouted and vigorously waved her hand to the waitress who had just approached the far end of the bar where Sara was headed. She stopped to see what drinks Molly needed for her table, so

Rebecca leapt at the opportunity to at least make contact.

"I'll come over in a minute." Molly's wave was less vigorous.

"Okay." Rebecca sat on her stool wondering what to say when Molly did come over. While she looked put together with her stylish pixie cut and required uniform top, she wasn't overly peppy or smiley. Was she upset about Max's death or was she the murderer?

Rebecca pondered how to approach Molly when she eventually arrived carrying the calamari order Sara had put in. "Here you go." She placed the plate with perfectly golden-fried rings next to a small plastic container of red spiciness. "Need anything else?"

"I wanted to check on you. How are you doing?"

Molly was completely caught off guard. She stuttered and stumbled through, "Um, why...would you say that?"

"I read about Max. You two were seeing each other, right?"

A voice hollered from the kitchen, "Molly, order up."

"I have to go get that, but I'll come back." Confusion painted itself all over her face, and her body started to move before her feet, almost causing her to trip. Rebecca grabbed Molly's arm and steadied her. "I'm okay. Thanks." She wandered back to the kitchen to grab another order.

That interaction did not go the way Rebecca would have scripted it. Molly now had time to think about her answer. If guilty, she had an excuse – work – to avoid

Rebecca, and the chance to come up with an alternate story.

Rebecca swiveled on her stool and started eating the calamari...delicious! The breading was crisp and flakey. It was clear this had been breaded here just before being dropped into the frier with a flour and cornmeal breading, not liquid – just the way Rebecca preferred. She wished The Catch of the Day could be open all year. Pacing herself would be important tonight as she may be here for a long time trying to catch up with Molly in between customers or, worst case scenario, not getting to really talk to her until the end of her shift.

Rebecca's fear came true. The rest of the night, Molly not only avoided all eye contact, but she also avoided her end of the bar entirely. It seemed like she was taking the long route to get to the kitchen every time, even though walking past her would have been easier and faster. Sara checked on Rebecca occasionally. Turns out, Sara just started a job bartending at The Steadfast, a local restaurant that was open all year at the other end of town. She agreed to cover a few nights she otherwise had off to help out Ben without hurting her full-time job security or Ben's feelings. He may have been a big pain in her backside, but he was still family and the one keeping an affordable roof over her head. Prior to this, Rebecca didn't think Sara had any bartending experience, so jumping straight into the deep end was her plan for the summer.

At one point, Rebecca finally caved and ordered a real dinner because this clearly wasn't going to be over soon. "Sara, could I order, please?"

"I thought you'd never ask." It was an attempt at humor that came off snarky. Rebecca knew she would need to leave a good tip for taking up a seat at the bar all night.

"Can I please get the grilled haddock platter, garlicy?"

"Side?"

Rebecca would not normally order this, but the oil-laden appetizer told her she needed to be careful with the amount of fried food in her dinner choice. "New potatoes, please."

"I'll put that in."

"Thanks." Now, more waiting. Rebecca spent the next hour or so trying to get Molly's attention. The few times she caught her eye, Molly hurried off, breaking the moment. When people started clearing out for the night – it wasn't the weekend after all – Molly finally came and sat on a stool next to Rebecca.

"That was a long time for calamari."

"I had fish after...now ice cream." Rebecca was slowly nursing the remains of a small scoop of frozen yogurt. If she wasn't careful, this investigation was going to cost her extra inches around her waist along with a lot of money.

"What do you know?"

Rebecca was prepared to take her shot. "I know you were seeing Max and that you accused him of at least flirting with someone else on Saturday night."

"We weren't telling anyone we were dating. Didn't want it to be an issue at work if he got drinks for me first or I helped him out when he got busy. It was new." Tears welled in her eyes, but she didn't let them fall.

"Sounds like half of the restaurant heard what you said, so I'm sure it's not a secret anymore. What happened that night?" Rebecca was just going to sit and listen as long as it took, even if she had to actively bite her lower lip to stop from interrupting.

"I watched Max flirt with most of the women at the bar. Tips, right? I got it, but this woman, he kept coming back to her even when she didn't need a drink. I'd seen her on multiple nights, so I couldn't hold back any longer. I yelled at him near the end of the night, and again while we were the only two closing, then I went for a run – a long run. It was pitch black by the time I got back, and Max's car was here, but I didn't see him at the bar so I figured he went home with her. I can't believe the last thing I ever said to him was an accusation." The tears broke through the surface tension and created tracks in her makeup, accompanied by sniffles and sobs.

Rebecca waited. She placed a hand on Molly's knee, but she waited.

"I got in my car and drove to his place, but no one was there, so I went home."

"Did you see anyone you knew on your run or anyone else after leaving the restaurant?" She couldn't stop herself. As soon as she said it, she regretted it. She just crossed a line between concerned friend and interviewer.

"Why? Trying to figure out if I did it? What is this?

57

Did you really stay here all night so you could ask me if I killed my boyfriend? If I killed Max?"

"No, not at all. I was worried that you were upset and had no one to comfort you." It was a good attempt to cover up her mistake, but Molly didn't buy it. If Rebecca had put herself in the position of interviewer, she might as well own it. "Donny was here Saturday night, and he said he offered Max a shot and Max took it. I didn't realize he was able to drink after what happened in high school. Know anything about that?" Fingers crossed, Rebecca waited again.

She let out a long sigh. "Max could drink, but only some alcohol. The intolerance was about histamines, so beer and wine were out of the question, but some hard liquor was okay. Occasionally he would sip something for the taste, but not whole drinks or to get drunk. Even a small amount made his face flush. Donny knew that. Why would he offer to buy Max a drink?"

"Donny said he offered him beer first. Do you think Donny had any reason to try to kill Max?"

In all of her reading, Rebecca couldn't think of a time where the word guffaw was more appropriate, but that is exactly what Molly did. "Did Donny have any reason to kill Max?" Molly sarcastically asked herself. "He had dozens, but they are all older than our high school diplomas. Every night Donny came in here drinking, he would start talking to Max about 'the good ole days' when they played basketball together or hung out at Wellington Beach in the summer, but the memories always took a turn the more Donny had to drink."

"How can a memory take a turn? It's a memory. If they were friends, wouldn't they have the same memories?"

"I never said they were friends. They hung out in the same circles but weren't really friends. Donny would start talking about the year they won the championship, and when it was Max's turn to talk, Donny would cut him off saying that he didn't get to play because Max hogged the spotlight. Max would try to change the subject, but Donny would start to complain that he could have made the 1000-point career list if Max would have passed more. It just devolved from there until someone would drive Donny home or call a friend to pick him up. Saturday night, Ben said Donny wasn't welcome back anymore after this time."

"Funny. Donny didn't mention that part. Wonder if he even knows. He said he doesn't remember how he got home or anything until the next morning."

"Oh, he knows now. Showed up here last night, and Ben kicked him out before he could even sit down. Lots of peacocking about how Ben didn't really mean it, and everything was fine. Said he was just blowing off steam. Ben told him in no uncertain terms to leave and never come back. Donny seemed angry and crushed at the same time."

So many new puzzle pieces were falling into place. Rebecca now wondered if Donny would really come back after killing Max, and did he return on the night in question in a drunken rage to kill Max because he did really know he had been thrown out for good? Kenny better have those fried pickles if he planned to get all of Rebecca's new information.

"Gosh, Molly, I'm so sorry you're going through all of this after losing Max."

"Thanks, and thanks for checking on me. I feel awful that the last friend he saw before he died was yelling at him. I'm sure you weren't really accusing me of anything, but I've just been so on edge trying to work here after leaving Saturday night so...unfinished."

What did she mean by unfinished? Rebecca felt bad for Molly, but that ending was so...vague. Did Molly mean there was unfinished business she had to take care of after everyone else or just the accusation of Max's flirting was unfinished.

"Well, I need to clean up and start the process of closing up the restaurant for the night." Molly stood. "Did you need anything else?"

"No. I'll settle up with Sara and be on my way. If you need anything, don't hesitate to stop in at the library. Seems like I'm always there."

"I appreciate it. Have a good night."

Molly walked off to do exactly as she said. Rebecca settled her tab and started a mental list of things Molly had confirmed and information that was new and troubling. It was getting late for Rebecca and for her two kitties waiting at home for her. After settling her bill and a big hug with Sara, she walked to her car. On the way, her phone vibrated. She took it out of her back pocket to check who was responsible for the alert.

Kenny: Pizza and Pickles tomorrow

Kenny: I'll be there at 7pm

Kenny: Mushrooms?

Rebecca: Yes, Yes and Yes, please

Kenny: Stay out of trouble until then

Rebecca: You too

She opened the door on the driver's side and landed with a grunt in the seat. She pulled the door closed and accepted the fact that she still required a physical key that turned to operate her car. A huge car payment wasn't too far in her future, but what she had was good enough for now.

The car practically drove itself back to her house along familiar roads. She trudged to the front door, letting herself in and dropping to the floor to be loved on by Joey and Bean. "Good evening, my kitties. Who's hungry?" A variety of noises and affectionate movements followed Rebecca to the cabinet and then the food dishes. She changed the water and headed up to bed. Solving a mystery certainly was exhausting. She looked at herself in the bathroom mirror when she got upstairs and smiled at the black t-shirt she wore which appropriately said, 'Easily Distracted by Cats and Books.' While getting ready for bed, she tried hard not to think about what she and Kenny would talk about tomorrow night so she could turn her brain off enough to fall asleep. After the second ten minutes of the recorded cooking competition show, she was out.

# Chapter 8

## *The Not-Date*

From her bedroom, Rebecca heard the front door open. She crept to the doorway and hovered just inside, listening for more sounds.

"Hey guys." Kenny's voice eased the knot in Rebecca's stomach. "I don't think you can have any of the food I brought." If Rebecca was lucky, that food would include fried pickles. It's not like she couldn't make them herself. She had, loads of times, just not actually fried. The substitute fried pickles she made at home were delicious, but tedious, and not the same as coming out of a deep frier. The sound of Kenny talking sweetly to her kitties made the butterflies in her stomach come alive. It really was quite comical and cliché to be referencing butterflies, even if only in her own head, after always rolling her eyes at that phrase in books. He didn't know she could hear him, and he was still the kind of man any woman could hope for.

"I'll be right down," she called down the stairs.

Rebecca turned from her bedroom door back to her closet. She was now on shirt number four of the getting dressed process. It was just Kenny. Why was she still getting dressed? He had seen her in PJs from several Christmases ago not a month earlier, and neither of them cared. Why was tonight different? "Remember, Rebecca, it's a not-date," she quietly scolded herself. She didn't want things to change between them, did she?

Keeping shirt number four on – a purple t-shirt featuring a line drawing of an open book with a fantasy scene developing from the pages – simply because changing again meant this was something more than the not-date she kept telling herself it was, she bounded down the stairs and around the corner into the kitchen. "Nice to see you have finally given up knocking."

"Well, someone told me about one hundred times I didn't need to anymore. I finally took the hint."

Was that the turning point? Did she tell him not to knock, and it was a subliminal message that this was now more than a platonic friendship. She shook off the thought and looked up. Kenny was examining her face.

"You okay? I really can knock. It doesn't bother me. I just thought..."

"No. I told you not to anymore because close friends don't need to." Rebecca threw out the word friend to see if she got a reaction.

Kenny seemed unphased by the statement and started to lay out paper plates and plastic utensils on the countertop. Rebecca looked around for the food and saw none.

"Did you get pizza?" How could an entire pizza be hidden? He clearly brought food because he mentioned it to Joey and Bean.

"Of course I did...and the fried pickles."

"Well, where is it?" She examined her clear counter-tops, the empty island and even the dining room table – nothing.

The *beep, beep, beep* of the oven told them both it had reached the desired temperature.

"I put it all in the oven to warm it up. Everything would get too soggy in the microwave."

Did he seriously just get better by the minute? How had all of the little gestures been missed these past few months? Maybe this was new, and she hadn't missed any signals. "That was a great idea. Thanks." She walked to the fridge to get drinks. There was the raspberry iced tea she loved – a single bottle. "What would you like to drink?"

"Just water, please. I know I haven't been doing a good job lately. There's always water in the cruiser with me, but I just never seem to get around to drinking it. I saw a water bottle online that has a sensor in it to remind you to drink with an app on your phone, but that seemed a bit much."

"Yeah, and expensive, I bet. Do you have to charge the water bottle?"

"I hadn't looked into it that far. Thought it was above my pay grade."

They both had a good chuckle about the water bottle with a phone app. "I really shouldn't tease," Rebecca admitted. "I have an automatically cleaning litter box for the kitties, and that has a phone app."

First Kenny stopped moving, then he gave her a very quizzical, brow-furrowed stare. "A what?"

"The litter box, it cleans itself when it gets used and sends me a text message when the tray needs to be emptied. Best money I ever spent on the kitties."

"Well, now I've heard it all." Kenny turned to the oven and, using an oven mitt, removed one cookie sheet with the pizza. However, he left a second in the oven with the fried pickles on it – two types of fried pickles. Rebecca snuck a look, just to see what kind. Karen wasn't going to let her hear the end of this...if she ever found out.

"Where did you find fried pickles?"

"Well, after some research, as any good police chief would do, I found that the pizza place had fried pickle spears and Jilly's had slices."

"But Jilly's closes at like two or three, doesn't it?"

"Yes. I put in an order before they closed and picked it up ten minutes later."

"Kenny, that was over four hours ago." Karen would *never* let this go now. Rebecca absolutely couldn't let her know about this big detail.

"I know. Kept them in the fridge at the station until it was time to leave, thus the oven. I only bought them because I didn't know if you liked the spears or the slices. I told you, research. Any good police chief would do the same."

Well, now Rebecca knew why she tried on four shirts. She looked down at the one she decided to settle on because it was physically on her body when Kenny got there. It wasn't a bad choice, but she wished she'd gone with number three now.

"Are we eating in front of the television or talking first, since I know why you wanted me here for pizza, and it wasn't for the pizza?" Was there a hint of a double meaning to that? Rebecca knew she needed to clear her head of any more distractions, and right now, Kenny was the distraction.

"Whatever could you mean, Chief Towne?" Rebecca sashayed her hips on the way to the fridge and fluttered an imaginary fan in front of her face like a southern belle. "Tonight's movie was going to be Sweet Home Alabama, but now it's your pick for bringing the pizza and pickles, and it's your choice for the order of the evening as well." When she paused long enough to realize just how flirty that was, she removed the water pitcher from the fridge as well as the ranch dressing and set them on the counter.

"I guess that means I skip the next movie night. Tonight, let's talk then watch." Kenny placed two pizza slices on each of their paper plates and went back to the oven to remove the pickles.

Rebecca watched as they completed such a domestic task together. She opened the ranch dressing and put some on her plate. If a jaw could literally hit the floor, Kenny's would have. She giggled as she slid the bottle over toward his plate. "This is the one and only acceptable use for ranch dressing."

Kenny stood in shocked silence, still holding the hot cookie sheet of fried pickles in his oven-mitted hand.

"What?" Rebecca went about retrieving a spatula to remove the pickles.

"I just can't believe I took that many months of ribbing over ranch dressing when you, yourself, actually eat it." He placed the cookie sheet on the stove top and turned off the oven while still thinking about the darn ranch dressing.

"I only use it to dip fried pickles into, so I eat it fewer than five times a year." She removed about half of the slices and one spear from the sheet and placed them on her plate with the pizza.

"Slices then. I'm glad I took the risk."

"I haven't made my mind up about the spears yet. I've never had them before."

Kenny plopped a dollop of ranch on his plate as well and took a couple of each type of pickle. "So, what do you think you know that I don't know about this murder."

"Are we calling it a murder now?" Holding her pizza like an imaginary cigar, she did her best Groucho Marx impression – it was pretty bad.

"Officially we are calling it a murder investigation."

"What *officially* changed that?" Rebecca continued to eat the fried pickle slices while Kenny spoke.

"I guess I'll go first." He took a bite of the pizza and thought about what he was going to say. "Off the record, Max was found to have over twice the legal alcohol limit in his system at the time of death. Now, that doesn't make it murder, but the next fact does. He was found in the water but with no water in his lungs. He didn't drown. Something killed him before he ended up in the water.

The reports came back that he had no food in his system. From our investigations, it seems he had worked all night Friday at the bar, crashed with Molly, woke up late Saturday morning and rushed off to The Catch of the Day. He worked a double, and I think you know how the evening part of the shift went. Now, spill the details you got." He reached over and swiped a bit of sauce from the corner of her mouth, wiping it off on a paper napkin before digging into his pickles.

"So, it seems that both Ben and Molly think they were the last one to see Max alive, though they have probably swapped stories by this point. Max's car was in the parking lot at the end of the night, so Molly thinks he went home with the woman from the bar, and Ben thinks he got a ride. Donny was permanently banned only to show back up because he was so drunk, he didn't know he had been kicked out for good. He didn't have any memories of how he got home or anything until the next morning, if he is to be believed."

"Do you believe him?"

"I think I do. His grudges are so old, I can't imagine murder suddenly being the result, and really, that night he should have been pissed at Ben, not Max. Donny just doesn't make sense as a viable suspect, but I wouldn't delete the file of information you have on him just yet."

"Why, thank you, Detective Ramsey." His sarcasm was followed by a quick wink. "Anything else?"

"Ben seemed very preoccupied by business details when I talked to him. If he murdered Max, he's doing a good job compartmentalizing his feelings. Molly seems devastated by the loss and angry at herself for how things ended. However, she could be feeling many of those same feelings if she were the killer or just the girlfriend who lost her boyfriend." Rebecca paused. "I guess that means I really don't have a strong feeling about Ben or Molly, though I really can't find a reason for Ben to kill Max."

"What if I told you Ben and Max had not been getting along well. Max wanted to take a bigger role in running the bar and asked Ben for a raise and new job title."

"That's not a reason to kill someone, especially someone you need in order for your restaurant to run."

"No, but Max was also threatening to take about half of the staff with him to another restaurant for the summer. His threats, if he followed through on them, would have really crippled Ben's chances for a successful season, and it's hard to turn a profit the first few years you open. One bad summer might mean Ben would have to sell the place."

"Well, that is something. Guess he's lucky he got Sara to fill in some shifts until he can find a replacement."

"Sara?" Kenny said around a bite of pizza. He stopped eating and looked up.

"Ben's little sister. She was a year behind us in school."

"I didn't know she started working there. I will add that to my do-not-delete files."

They both waited and chewed for a bit, throwing glances at each other and then turning back to their dinners. "Do you plan on telling Karen that I brought fried pickles?"

The once pale cheeks turned a warm pink as Rebecca replied, "Nope. She doesn't need to know that you brought the pickles."

"And if she asks?"

A zipping motion across Rebecca's lips revealed she was not planning on saying anything...and she wasn't, was she?

"Well, if you can keep that secret, you best be able to keep this next one. The really puzzling thing to come from the report is that he had no solid food in his stomach, probably because he woke late and went straight to work after a double on Friday and then worked a double before his death. The only thing found in his stomach was alcohol and trace amounts of egg."

"Egg but no solids? That's odd."

"We haven't confirmed it, but best we can figure, he was using raw eggs for some kind of workout program that had a diet component. We just got the report today, so we haven't had a chance to ask anyone about that possibility."

"Kenny, he was allergic to eggs, wasn't he? Don't you remember when he was in fourth grade and was taken by ambulance from the school? They learned that he had a bunch of allergies."

"Yeah, but we knew about the alcohol intolerance, and whiskey was one alcohol that was pretty safe for him, historically anyway."

"Right, but another one was eggs. He could eat things

like cookies that had eggs baked into them, but not straight scrambled or fried..." Rebecca was interrupted.

"Or raw. If he was allergic to eggs, there is no way he would have done a diet that required eating or drinking eggs like that."

"Exactly."

Kenny stood and started to look around. "Do you mind if we cut tonight short? I need to get back to the station and review my notes from earlier this week."

"Of course not. Before you leave, you should know that I had just discussed Max's allergy story with Ben on Tuesday. He very clearly recalled the story about Max getting taken by ambulance for an allergic reaction in the fourth grade, and he was the one to bring it up."

"Thanks for that information." Kenny was already moving in the direction of the front door.

Rebecca quickly grabbed a box of aluminum foil from a drawer and wrapped up two slices of pizza for Kenny to take with him. "Here. You'll want to make sure you eat more since you really didn't get dinner." She had followed him to the front door.

"It was worth it. Hope you liked the pickles." Her hand briefly brushed his as she handed over the foil-wrapped leftovers. There was no spark as they were both so fully wrapped up in details of this new discovery.

Kenny bent down to put on his shoes. "Have a good night." He opened and closed the door faster than Rebecca could respond. Now there was no chance she was going to sleep one wink, and she had to work tomorrow.

# Chapter 9

## *The Whodunnit*

WHILE HER BODY WAS IN A HORIZONTAL POSITION for most of the night, Rebecca didn't get so much as a catnap over the last eight hours. She gave up around 4am and started cleaning, reviewing all of the information that had been swimming around in her head. She decided to text Kenny around 5am, though she didn't expect a response for several more hours.

Rebecca: Any more developments last night?

Three dots immediately popped up. She stared at the screen while pausing the current cleaning project – a deep clean of the guest bathroom downstairs.

Kenny: Not so much progress as a plan.

Kenny: Can you meet me at The Catch for lunch at 11?

Rebecca: Mary comes in to volunteer today. I'll ask if she can cover me.

Kenny: Let me know as soon as she gets there, K?

Rebecca: Will do, Chief.

While Rebecca was the only librarian on the payroll, she had a few different volunteers who could step in to give her a break when needed. Mary would probably be fine to cover, so long as she showed up. Rebecca never wanted her to feel like it was a job, rather, a hobby. She loved and appreciated the grandmotherly qualities she saw in Mary. The library was one of the things that gave her purpose, having been retired for so long now. Tea with the ladies was nice, but feeling useful had its benefits on the brain and soul as well.

Rebecca wasn't needed at the library until ten, and cleaning the bathroom would only distract her for so long, so she got ready for the day. Her kitties were so confused when she fed them early, vowing to stop by the house for treats after lunch and before returning to the library. They got extra snuggles before she loaded up the green Subaru for a day of uncertainty.

The library had never been so clean or organized on a Friday morning before opening to the public. There wasn't a single fingerprint smudge or cobweb that had snuck by the efficiency of a woman who wanted the time to pass by like Rebecca did today. When Mary showed up at 11am, the door hadn't even fully closed before she was practically attacked by a rambling Rebecca.

"Morning, Mary. Hey, just wondering if you would mind if I stepped out for lunch today? Chief Towne has something going on at The Catch of the Day regarding the investigation and asked this morning if I'd join him at lunch time. I mean, if you don't mind, I'd really appreciate it."

"Slow down, dear, and good morning. Something about lunch, that handsome Chief Towne and the investigation. What else was there?"

Rebecca took a deep breath and relieved Mary of the bag she was carrying. They both walked over to the desk where she offered a seat to the woman she hoped would acquiesce to her request. "Mary, I already checked in all of the books from the drop and cleaned everything I could see that needed cleaning, and some areas that didn't. The children's section is in good shape, and there is no paperwork nor mailings to deal with."

"Dear, what time did you get in this morning?" Mary placed a concerned hand on Rebecca's arm.

"I was here just after 6am, but that's beside the point." Rebecca was still speaking quite quickly, but she was easier to understand now and stopped to take the occasional breath.

"Well, dear, this lunch must be very important. What did you say was the reason? You don't often take a lunch like that on a Friday."

"I know, and all I'll ask is that you check in and out books of patrons that come in while I'm gone, nothing else. Chief Towne asked if I would join him at The Catch of the Day at lunch time, eleven specifically, and that it had to do with the investigation into Max's death, but no details. Would you mind terribly if I went?" Rebecca would physically be on her knees if she thought it would help, but her hands were in a sort of praying position, subconsciously hoping for a positive outcome to an otherwise reasonable request.

"Of course, I don't mind. I've never said no before; why would I start now?" She smiled at Rebecca, allowing her stomach full of butterflies to settle.

"I didn't think you would, but it seems like this could be a really big deal. I didn't sleep a wink last night."

"But you said Chief Towne didn't ask you until this morning."

"That's correct." Time for Rebecca to figure out another reason for not sleeping, or she could choose to tell Mary the truth. Truth. "Last night, I was speaking with Chief Towne about some new developments, so I was thinking about those until I heard from him again this morning." Half of the truth would have to do. Mary didn't need to know he came over for pizza and brought fried pickles.

"Well, you still have fifty-five minutes before you need to be there. Anything I can do to help you until then?"

Mary was the sweetest woman. Rebecca would have to remember to bring something back for her if time allowed. "I'll keep tidying up other genres if you want to sit at the desk."

"Nah. I'll be at the desk while you're gone, so I'll tackle the New Release section. This way, I can still hear if anyone comes in."

"Thanks." Rebecca went to the back of the library to work on Historical Fiction after setting an alarm on her phone to go off at 10:45am. This left her enough time to get to her car, manage the one traffic light between the library and The Catch of the Day and find parking. She could walk in, calm and collected, and ready for whatever Chief Towne needed from her.

A quick farewell to Mary sent Rebecca down the stairs to the lower parking lot to get into her car as quickly as possible when her phone alarm rang. The solitary traffic light was green, so she reached the restaurant with time to spare. There were spots in the back where the employees parked, so she took one of those, not wanting to take the good spots away from paying patrons should this be over quickly. Chief Towne's cruiser was also parked in the back, only closer to the side where people lined up for the take-out window. She noticed that he backed into his spot. '*Just like any good police officer would,*' she could hear him say in her head.

A vibration alerted her to an incoming text message.

Kenny: Take a seat at the bar when you get here.

Kenny: Don't talk to me. Just listen.

Rebecca chose not to respond. When she got inside, she took a seat at the bar as directed. She didn't need to know the *why* because she trusted his intuition. Not two minutes later, she heard Kenny, Donny and Ben talking off to her left.

"So, we've known each other for a long time, right? I was hoping that I could mediate the possibility of Donny being allowed back here under a probationary sort of arrangement. I've spoken to both of you recently due to Max's death, and I'd hate to see more of our graduating class alienated by this distressing event. What do you say, Ben? Is there any scenario where you could see Donny being allowed to come back?"

Rebecca snuck glances over her shoulder to see how the two men were reacting to Kenny's proposal when Molly came around the corner. "What are you doing back in here?" she lashed out in the direction of the three men.

Donny's face lit up with wide eyes and an open mouth. "Huh?" He looked shocked at the attack from Molly.

"You're the reason Max is dead. You two got into that stupid fight over drinks, and you came back and killed him, didn't you?" She got right up in Donny's face with a stiff pointer finger mere millimeters from the center of his nose.

"I was too drunk to even make it home. I didn't come back, and I didn't kill Max. I hardly made it into the shop the next morning. And you can ask Ben who drove me home because I don't know that either."

Kenny decided to intervene. Clearly, he hadn't planned on Molly being there to add her two cents. "Alright, alright. Molly, maybe you should cool off in the back."

"Yes, Molly," Ben interrupted, "you should go cool off. The freezer is available if you don't want to be in the employee parking lot. Either way, don't come back until you can be civilized."

Angry tears streamed down her face as she bolted around the bar and out the back door. She nearly ran into Sara on her way out.

"What's going on? I went up to my apartment for a minute and came back to a crying waitress and the police chief with a banned patron hanging around my bar." Sara's blonde hair was half pulled up on top of her head to keep it out of her face while the back hung straight and ended above her shoulders. "Seriously, why is Donny here?"

"Well, if you must know, I'm trying to talk to Ben about letting Donny come back, unless you have a reason he shouldn't."

"Nope, no skin off my nose." Sara put her head down and puttered around behind the bar while Rebecca watched but continued to listen to Kenny.

"Ben, what do you say?" Kenny attempted to start up the negotiations again.

Ben scratched his temple. "Donny, what happens if we have another issue like Saturday night? What if it's my sister behind the bar when you get belligerent?"

"I'll agree to a maximum, even if it's not what you require of everyone else. I just want to be able to have somewhere to hang out, especially in the summer." Donny stared into Ben's eyes and when Ben didn't answer quickly, he looked down at his sandaled feet. "I get it. I'm a risk you can't take. I'm sorry." Donny turned to walk away when Ben called him back.

"Alright. Two-drink maximum for now until we see if it's you or the alcohol that's the problem, and no showing up already drunk or I'll kick you out immediately. Deal?"

"Deal." The men shook on it and came in for one of those half-hugs where they slapped each other's backs twice then backed away from each other.

Rebecca had been waiting for something to strike.

Kenny had to have brought her here for a reason. She had been up all night thinking and looking things up on her phone. There must have been a reason for him to request to meet here then not even talk to her. He specifically told her to sit at the bar. Was it about the proximity to the discussion or the location specifically?

"Now, gentlemen, I'm on duty, so there's no off time for me, but I know Donny has coverage at The Lakehouse and Ben is here at my request, so I'm sure the two of you could at least talk over lunch, right?"

While the two men thought about Kenny's newest proposal, Rebecca's metaphorical light-bulb moment finally clicked. "Sara, can I get a whiskey sour?"

Sara turned to eye Rebecca quizzically. "It's Friday afternoon. Isn't the library open?"

"Yes, but I have a lunch break and plan to order lunch as well. Is the bar open for business?" Rebecca didn't drink alcohol, but no one else needed to know that right now.

"Of course." Sara busied herself with collecting the correct glass and searching for something under the bar. "Ben, where are the eggs?"

"For the record, they are in the walk-in cooler, but why do you need eggs?"

"Rebecca ordered a whiskey sour."

"Bourbon, lemon juice, simple syrup. What kind of bartender's black book are you using?" Ben was visibly confused.

"Sara, where were you the night Max was murdered,

after closing?" Kenny asked while he walked over to the bar, blocking the only potential exit for Sara.

"What? Why do you ask?"

"Do you have an alibi?" His body occupied the open space normally used by the bartender to enter and exit their work area, the wooden surface sat opened like half of a drawbridge.

"I was in my apartment. Why?"

"So, you don't have an alibi?" At some point, during this line of questioning, Molly had returned from the employee parking lot, and Ben was closing in on Kenny's personal space.

"Chief Towne, what kind of question is that? Why are you asking my sister if she has an alibi?" Ben started to look both angry and nervous as his gaze shifted between Kenny and Sara.

"I have reason to believe that Sara killed Max on Saturday night after Molly left for her run and while you were preoccupied closing up in the back. Sara, I'd be happy to read you your rights before heading straight to the station."

Everyone was silent. The restaurant was far from packed this early on a Friday morning, but the shouting and police presence had caught the attention of the patrons already starting their weekends.

"Seriously, why would I kill Max?" Sara shifted her weight while rotating her head between Ben and Kenny. "Max was a great guy. Why would I kill him?"

"That's what I'm asking you. Might it have anything to do with Molly? Or Ben?"

Sara tried to jump over the bar and make a run for it, but Kenny quickly stopped her by pressing her into the floor and hand cuffing her behind her back. "You have the right to remain silent. Anything you say can and will be used against you in a court of law. You have the right to an attorney. If you cannot afford an attorney, one will be appointed for you before any questioning." He carefully helped Sara back to her feet. Two other officers had joined him and were watching Ben to see if he was going to react to this now tense situation. They must have been just out of eyesight as this was the first time Rebecca noticed two large men in full uniform. "Do you have any questions, Sara?"

Sara whipped her head around. "Rebecca, why did you order that drink?"

"We were just kids on the playground the day Max was taken away in the ambulance. We all heard him relive the details of the ride and stay in the hospital that involved allergy testing. There really wasn't much that came up, but we all heard that eggs were on the short list. Being the children that we were, everyone was either worried about him dying or curious about what could really hurt him again if they wanted to get back at him for something childish. Ben and Donny were also there. I didn't really think of you as a suspect, at first. Plenty of people knew about Max's allergies."

Rebecca stood from the stool she had been occupying throughout this whole event. "I knew you had been studying for your new job bartending, and I recently learned that whiskey sours were traditionally made with egg whites, though the practice isn't all that common anymore. Last night, while I was looking up drinks that contain egg, the whiskey sour popped up as the most plausible since Ben had told me he'd shared whiskey with Max the night he died. You would have known that Max was allergic, and a drink containing eggs would be easy to swap out after he had already been drinking earlier in the night because he was distraught about Molly yelling at him."

"Max was distraught?" Molly spoke for the first time since returning to the restaurant, and Rebecca decided for the second time this week to just listen and wait.

Sara turned – her shoulders and head the only movable parts of her body – to glare at Molly. "Max and I had been a thing until he started working here. You came along, and he broke it off with me shortly after. I'd been talking to Max about getting back together, and he said he was falling in love with you. He didn't want me trying to rekindle something that wasn't there anymore." This time it was Sara with the angry tears. "I loved him! I wanted to marry him, and he wanted you!"

Kenny decided it was time to remove Sara from the restaurant and officially charge her with Max's murder. Rebecca remained at the restaurant, knowing she wouldn't hear from Kenny for a while now that Sara was in custody. Customers at tables returned to eating their lunches, and Donny excused himself quietly with a half wave to Rebecca. Ben remained in place, staring at nothing in particular.

"Ben, is there anything I can do?" Rebecca, always

the helper, offered without any sort of idea what she could possibly do to help this situation. Ben just watched his sister confess to the murder of his childhood friend. What could Rebecca provide?

"No. I think I'll just have to figure this one out on my own this time, but thanks for the offer." He quietly shuffled off to the kitchen leaving Rebecca standing on her own near the bar. The other police officers had left with the chief, and Rebecca realized she still had to return to the library.

"Rebecca," Molly whispered as she touched her arm, causing Rebecca to jump. "What do we do now?"

She hadn't realized Molly was still waiting quietly near the employee entrance. "Well, we let the police do their job."

"I mean, how do we move on?" Molly looked empty, her face paler than usual with dark circles under her eyes. The realization that she wasn't the only one to suffer a great loss was visible in every blink of her eyes and uncontrolled movement of her body.

"I'll go let Ben know I'm driving you home before I return to the library, okay?" She ushered Molly to a bar stool and made sure she was solid before leaving the dining space and entering the kitchen. She told Ben Molly needed to go home and he understood, though Rebecca could hear him panicking about losing his bartender and a waitress on a Friday afternoon while she was returning to help Molly.

Rebecca did just what she planned. She dropped Molly off on her way to the library but made sure to call

Molly's mom from the driveway before pulling out. Molly was going to need some support to make it through the next few days. Information traveled fast around the lake, and the newspaper was sure to carry the follow-up headlines to help sales. She even remembered her deal to give Bean and Joey a quick visit with treats and some attention. All within an hour, Rebecca was walking back through the doors of the library.

"Rebecca, dear, how did it go?" Mary looked up from the mystery novel she was reading behind the desk when Rebecca reached the lobby.

"Well, I helped solve a murder."

"Very good, dear. Very good."

# Chapter 10

## *The Epilogue*

Saturday morning at the library could really go either way depending on the weather. When the weather was pleasant, Rebecca could go a whole day without seeing a single patron. A cold or rainy day meant a constant flow of traffic, mostly children with a parent. Today was perfect for being outside, and Rebecca was stuck inside. After all of her cleaning yesterday morning, there wasn't much to do. She scrolled through the most recent posts from a number of bookstagramers she followed, hoping to discover new indie authors she could feature at the library. Even if she just recommended them when people were browsing, they might find a new author to support and fall in love with.

When the door opened, she was caught off guard. In strode Kenny with his two children, Megan and Melanie. Starting their names with the same letter had been the idea of his ex-wife, and he went along with it. They were two lovely girls who enjoyed reading and spending time in the library. However, it was surprising to see them on such a gorgeous June day after a long, dark winter. As soon as Rebecca waved and greeted the trio, the girls took off to the children's section.

"So, this is where the victorious celebrate after their triumph?" Kenny chuckled at his attempt to imitate a chivalrous knight harkening from the times of King Arthur in a deep bow.

"You get all of the glory, and well-deserved glory at that. You closed that case in a week with almost no evidence to start with. You should be very proud of yourself. I know the girls are too young to understand, but they would be so impressed by what a great job their dad did." The blush on Kenny's cheeks did not go unnoticed.

"Rebecca, please understand that without your *help* and first-hand knowledge of Max's health, this could have gone unsolved. I know that. We all thought he was drinking eggs for protein shakes and would never have connected that detail to a drink at the bar. Come on. Who puts eggs in drinks other than eggnog?"

"After my 'research' in the middle of the night, I learned about many drinks that include egg. Did you want to know some others?"

Kenny shook his head. "I'm all set. We just stopped in so I could say thank you. I couldn't have done it without you. You played your part at the restaurant perfectly."

"Wait. Did you know it was a whiskey sour when you asked me to meet you there?" Rebecca tilted her head and slightly squinted her eyes.

"I knew you were the only person who had as much if not more information than I had. I wanted to get Donny and Ben in the same place, hoping they might confess or slip up on some detail, and I needed you to hear it all in case we needed to have pizza and pickles again." This time it was Rebecca who blushed. Even though she knew Karen wasn't in the library, she still looked in the direction she had previously been for the original pizza and pickle conversation.

"What I'm trying to say, Rebecca," he spoke in a way that redirected her focus on him, "is that I didn't have a clue it was Sara. Even Molly's presence was a variable I couldn't control. When she burst in, yelling at Donny, I couldn't have written a more perfect storm. Getting our three lead suspects confronting each other in an emotionally charged atmosphere was gold. It made me even more thankful for your participation when I really hadn't given you any information to go on."

Rebecca smiled and confessed, "I wasn't completely sold on Sara."

"Who did you think it was?"

"I was equally confident it could have been Ben or Molly, but I was pretty sure about the drink. Either one could have been the last to see Max alive based on their stories. And what they told you was consistent with what they told me. Both Donny and Ben had confirmed that whiskey was safe for Max, so a whiskey sour was the only drink that fit your stomach content puzzle. Here's where the tricky part came in. If neither Ben nor Molly had a motive to kill, who did?"

"Plenty have killed for a lot less than a cheating boyfriend."

"Yeah, but I talked to Molly, and I just couldn't make it fit. When I ordered the whiskey sour, I wanted to see if it got a reaction from anyone. I only wished I could have told you before so we both could have been looking for reactions. I got lucky. Molly had no reaction and Sara basically gave me her confession. I only started to suspect her because she would have been studying bartending books to start her new job before adding on a few shifts to help out Ben. Not everyone knows a whiskey sour can contain egg, but being such a new study, it would have come up in her books."

"Between you and me," Kenny said quietly after approaching the check-out desk, "Sara confessed to everything once we got her back to the station. She got Max to drink a couple of the whisky sours with egg in them then convinced him he needed to get some air when he started to struggle. She walked him out to the end of the dock where they sat down together. When he stopped breathing, she simply pushed him off the end. I don't know where she thought his body would go, but she's going to be in prison for a long time. It sounds like we both got lucky." This confession, in such close proximity, was followed by an awkward silence broken by the return of Kenny's kids.

"Dad, we picked out two books each, just like you told us."

"We're ready to go." They were bouncing on the balls of their feet, ready to get on with their next adventure.

"Please put the books up on the counter so Ms. Rebecca can check them out."

While efficiently scanning and stamping the inside covers, she reminded them to come back often to get new books during the summer.

"Speaking of summer, the girls are out of school next week, so I'll be spending more time with them at my place. Don't be offended if I'm a bit busier..."

"Say no more. We'll chat again when we have time."

Kenny reminded the girls, "Say thank you to Ms. Rebecca."

"Thank you, Ms. Rebecca," they sang in unison.

"And thank you again, Ms. Rebecca, for all of your help." Kenny escorted the girls out of the library and as they passed by the windows, heading to the car, Rebecca gave a small wave in their direction.

She hoped it was just a 'see you later,' not goodbye. She didn't predict her feelings taking this turn, but she kind of wanted to see where it led. With Kenny having an ex and kids, it made things more complicated. Spending extra time this summer with his girls meant Rebecca could take some time to focus on herself. She was intent on making the most of this summer of discovery and picked up a brand-new cozy mystery, determined to finish it today or tonight, depending on where the afternoon took her. Besides, she could now consider this genre research instead of just reading for pleasure. She cracked the book open, having not even labeled it for the shelves, and began.

# PLEASE LEAVE A REVIEW!

★ ★ ★ ★ ★

## Virginia K Bennett

### An Appetite for Solving Crime

THANK YOU FOR READING MY BOOK!

I WOULD LOVE TO READ YOUR FEEDBACK ON
FACEBOOK, INSTAGRAM, AMAZON, OR
SIMPLY SEND AN EMAIL TO:
authorvirginiakbennett@gmail.com

# Also by Virginia K. Bennett

## The Mysteries of Cozy Cove

# Recipe

<u>Meatballs</u>

Ingredients:

1/2 lb ground pork

1/2 lb ground beef

1/2 lb ground lamb

1/2 cup finely grated Parmesan

1 large egg

1 1/2 tsp dried basil

1 1/2 tsp dried oregano

1 1/2 tsp dried Italian seasoning

1 tsp garlic powder

1 tsp salt

1/3 cup breadcrumbs

Additional 1/3 cup breadcrumbs

Additional 1/4 cup finely grated Parmesan

Preheat oven to 425 degrees.

In a large mixing bowl, combine the pork, beef, lamb, Parmesan, egg, basil, oregano, Italian Seasoning, garlic powder, salt and breadcrumbs. Using your hands, mix ingredients until well incorporated, but do not overmix. If the mixture is too wet, add additional breadcrumbs 1/4 cup at a time.

In a small bowl, combine additional breadcrumbs and Parmesan. Using your hands, shape the meatballs into rounds and roll in the additional breadcrumb mix. Place each meatball in individual mini-muffin tin holes. Bake for 20 minutes or until golden brown and cooked through. Turn after 10 minutes.

No cooking spray needed.

If desired, meatballs can be cooked in a crockpot with homemade sauce on low for a minimum of five hours. However, cooking times may vary depending on how much sauce and size of crockpot.

## About the Author

When she's not writing on her couch with her two cats, Twyla and Geo, Virginia is busy teaching middle school math, grocery shopping, cooking or spending time with her husband and son. Together, her small family loves to go geocaching and visit theme parks.

Mysteries have always been an interesting challenge for Virginia, much like watching a magician perform. Unless you want to hear the entire thought process behind who she thinks is the killer and why, you might want to avoid watching any movies together.

The path to publishing a book is different for everyone and her path is full of twists and turns. Thank you to those who support the journey.

facebook.com/VirginiaKBennett

instagram.com/authorvkbennett

Made in United States
North Haven, CT
19 October 2023

42929255R00059